# The Eagle and the Pelican

# The Eagle and the Pelican

DAVID GRETCH

Illustrations by Robin K. Gulack

In the beginning, before all that now exists,
there was an Eagle and a Pelican.

Some say it was Eagle who came first, while others say it was Pelican who came first.

Mostly, women believe Pelican came first, while most men believe it was Eagle who came first.

Eagle loved Pelican, and Pelican loved Eagle.

One day, Pelican filled her beak with eight smaller eagles, which she had made in Eagle's likeness, for she loved Eagle so much. She flew proudly across the sky with the smaller eaglets in her softly cushioned orange and yellow beak.

Soon Pelican came to the mountains, and she dropped two eaglets from her beak. They became Moose, Ruler of the mountains, and Elk, Moose's medicine animal.

Ever since then, Moose and Elk have ruled over and cared for all the creatures of the mountains.

The next day, Pelican flew over the Great Plains, and dropped a pair of eaglets from her beak, down to the prairie below, where the eaglets turned into Buffalo, King of the prairie, and Buffalo's medicine animal, Wolf.

Ever since then, Buffalo and Wolf have ruled over and cared for all the creatures of the Great Plains.

The following day, Pelican flew over the oceans, and dropped a pair of eaglets into the clear blue water below, where they turned into Orca, King of the ocean, and Orca's medicine animal, Walrus.

Ever since then, Orca and Walrus have ruled over and cared for all the creatures of the oceans.

On the following day, Pelican, realizing she had only two more eaglets in her beak, flew long and far, searching for the best place to drop the darlings.  Finally, as she became tired, she chose a beautiful, blue lake, and dropped the remaining two eaglets. One eagle landed in the lake, while the other missed the target (due to Pelican's fatigue) and landed in a river that was flowing away from the lake.  The eaglet that landed in the lake turned into Otter, the medicine animal of the lake.

The eaglet that landed in the river turned into Salmon, who was supposed to be King of the lake.  Salmon knew he belonged in the lake. However, he was too tired from the long flight to swim upstream. Instead, Salmon swam in the easier direction, the wrong direction.  Eventually, Salmon floated merrily down steam and into the ocean.

In the ocean, Salmon was quite happy and quickly multiplied to great numbers. With his many, many offspring, Salmon was delighted with the vastness of the ocean.  Soon enough, however, the ocean's King, Orca, found out about Salmon. Being of immense appetite, and naturally curious as well, Orca ate one Salmon, and found it more delicious than any food he had ever tasted.  He then ate another Salmon, and another, and soon all the Orcas were eating the Salmon, and other sea animals began eating Salmon, such as shark and Sea Lion, and even baby seals chased the weary Salmon.

Orca, being very wise, soon realized that the feast was too festive. Salmon would soon be all gone, so a decree was sent out that no more Salmon should be eaten.  Then, Orca went to Walrus, his medicine animal, to ask for help. Orca explained that Salmon were a beautiful new member of the ocean community, and that they tasted delicious.

Walrus tried one, and declared wholeheartedly to Orca, "Salmon truly are beautiful, and delicious too!"

Quickly, Orca warned Walrus not to eat any more Salmon, because their numbers were being depleted.  Orca admitted he felt guilty for having eaten so many of the beautiful Salmon himself.

Walrus then declared to Orca," As medicine animal of the ocean, I will try and fix the problem of the Salmon being depleted."

Walrus then went over to Salmon and asked, "Hi Salmon". And before Salmon could answer, Walrus asked, "Where do you come from, beautiful fish?".  Salmon replied,

"From the river".  Then Walrus told Salmon, "Go swim back up the river, and ask your Creator to send back many more Salmon to the ocean".

So, Salmon swam back up the river, and in the process, began to lay eggs, lots of eggs.

Then, just before dying, Salmon recognized the lake from which he had came, and looked up and saw soaring proudly, the Eagle and the Pelican high in the sky. They were pleased that Salmon had worked so hard to return to the lake

Many Salmon were born from the eggs that had been laid in the river.  The new salmon instinctively returned to the ocean, just as their parents had, eating worms and such, smelling the beautiful fragrances of Mother Nature, and stopping to memorize all interesting landmarks, all along the way.

When the new Salmon found the ocean, they were delighted by the beautiful colors. In the end, there were many, many, many Salmon in the ocean.

The return of such enormous numbers of Salmon to the ocean delighted both Orca and Walrus.  However, Orca remained careful not to eat too many Salmon, and every fall, Walrus instructs Salmon to swim back up the river and have more Salmon sent back to the ocean by Creator.

This is why Salmon swim up the river every fall, and down the river every spring.

END